Kate Temple

For every kid who's ever had their
lunch stolen by an ibis—Kate and Jol

To Niharika, thank you for making
our nest wonderful—Ronojoy and Shay

Scholastic Press
An imprint of Scholastic Australia Pty Limited (ABN 11 000 614 577)
PO Box 579 Gosford NSW 2250
www.scholastic.com.au

Part of the Scholastic Group
Sydney • Auckland • New York • Toronto • London • Mexico City
New Delhi • Hong Kong • Buenos Aires • Puerto Rico

Published by Scholastic Australia in 2020.
Text copyright © Kate and Jol Temple, 2020.
Illustrations copyright © Ronojoy Ghosh, 2020.

Kate and Jol Temple assert their moral rights as the authors of this work.
Ronojoy Ghosh asserts his moral rights as the illustrator of this work.

ISBN: 978-1-74383-004-8

 A catalogue record for this
book is available from the
National Library of Australia

Typeset in OllieFat.

Ronojoy Ghosh created these illustrations digitally.

Printed in China by RR Donnelley.
Scholastic Australia's policy, in association with RR Donnelley, is to use papers that are renewable and made
efficiently from wood grown in responsibly managed forests, so as to minimise its environmental footprint.

10 9 8 7 6 5   21 22 23 24 / 2

KATE AND JOL TEMPLE

BIN
CHICKEN

ILLUSTRATED BY
RONOJOY GHOSH

A Scholastic Press book from Scholastic Australia

In an ancient land, many moons ago,
where Pharaohs rule and palm trees grow,
lived a **sacred bird** with feathers all white,
an elegant beak and wings of a kite.

She sunned herself on the banks of the Nile . . .

But today she sits . . .

. . . on a **rubbish pile.**

Diving in dumpsters, traipsing through trash,
rummaging through rubbish, making
a **splash!**

Feasting on fish heads and day-old chips,
nibbling on nachos and orange pips,
banana peels, bubble gum, fried chicken legs,
fairy floss, toffee apples,
old curried eggs!

'Disgusting!' tweets Sparrow. 'Rats of the sky.'
But Ibis can't hear him with her head in a pie.

'Revolting!' adds Pigeon, as Ibis dives in
and pulls out a shiny bottle-top ring.

Crow makes a grimace, he's starting to sicken.
'Trash Turkey! Dumpster Duck!
Bin Chicken!'

Pigeon snorts, 'Don't go through that **trash!**
Can't you see it will give you a rash?'

'Agreed,' says Sparrow, 'it's hardly discerning.
And you **smell bad!** It's very concerning.'

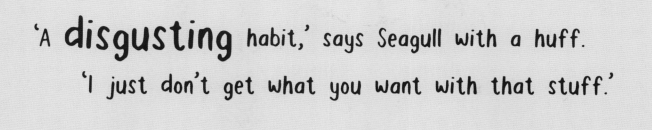

'A **disgusting** habit,' says Seagull with a huff.
'I just don't get what you want with that stuff.'

'True, true,' squawks Crow, 'that's not worth a thing.
Plastic beads, pipe cleaners, **violin string?!**'

'It's time you took off. Time to make tracks.
Stop wading through **rubbish** and worthless knick-knacks.

So, **buzz off!** Get out. You heard us! **Scram!**
It's embarrassing . . . and you smell like old ham.'

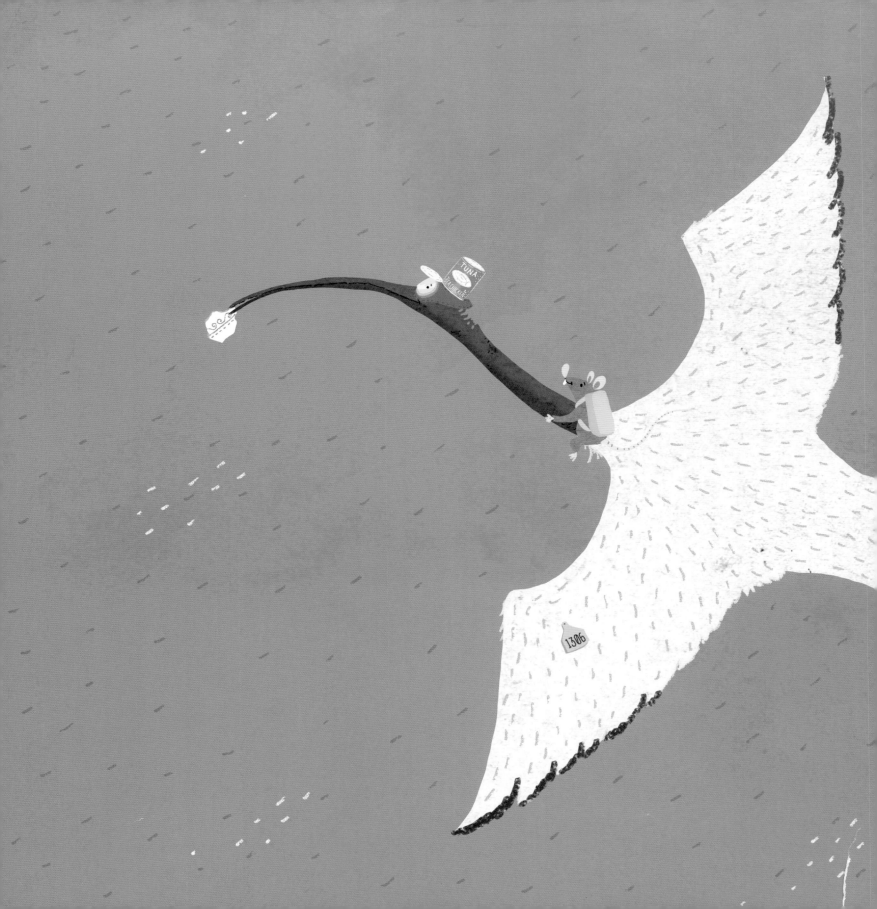

Ibis isn't ruffled, she just takes to the sky,
the stench from her wings is her only reply.

She soars over the city
and lands without grace

on a palm in a park,

her own **special** place.

Pie tins and bike wheels dazzle the eye,
and **shine** like a lighthouse up in the sky.

Wind chimes, lost socks, an old party hat,
broken sunglasses . . . even half a doormat.

At the heart of this nest, in a dirty, old town,
are soft, fluffy **chicks** all covered in down.

Ibis flutters her feathers and flaps her wings loudly.

She holds her head up as she says to them proudly,

'We've learned how to thrive in stormwater drains,
at bus stops and car parks and narrow back lanes.

These long, bony feet, once made for wading,
now make fine stilts for garbage-bin raiding.

And having no feathers up on our heads
was perfect for sifting the old riverbeds.

But it works just as well for sticking them in
and pulling out scraps from the rubbish bin.

We've swapped our swamps for the streets of the city,
and you'll meet many who think that's a pity.

They'll call you Bin Chicken, a foul dumpster diver.
But always remember . . .
you're a **survivor.**

So flap your smelly feathers, hold your head high,
chase down hot chips . . .

and always

follow that pie.'